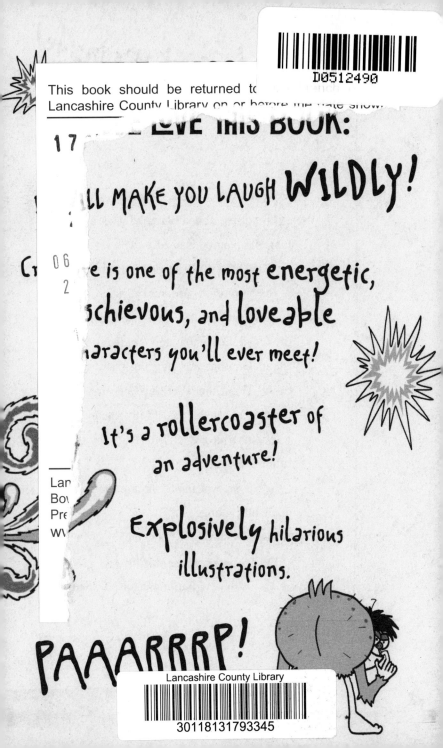

...LOVE THIS BOOK:

...'LL MAKE YOU LAUGH **WILDLY!**

...e is one of the most **energetic, mischievous,** and **loveable** ...characters you'll ever meet!

It's a **rollercoaster** of an adventure!

Explosively hilarious illustrations.

PAAARRRP!

Barnaby squawked. 'Gerroff!'

Creature grabbed Barnaby's ears and swung himself up onto his head.

'YOOOWWWW!' howled Barnaby.

Every one of Creature's hairs stood on end. He shot off Barnaby's head like a rocket-propelled hedgehog and landed on a huge chandelier that was hanging right above the train. The chandelier lurched dangerously. Creature chattered crossly at Barnaby.

'My ears have stretched!' Barnaby groaned, rubbing them.

'It's your own fault!' Nora exclaimed. 'You made him change . . . '

Barnaby shrugged. 'Blah blah—'

Creeeeeeeeeeeeeeeeakkkkkkk . . .

' . . . blah . . . ' Barnaby's voice trailed away.

He stared up at the swaying chandelier.

'What's that?' Nora rubbed her eyes. Jake coughed. Bits of plaster were falling on his head. He looked back up, and sucked his breath in sharply.

Creature's weight was too much for the chandelier. Slowly but surely, it was ripping out of the ceiling.

To Mum. For letting me run wild but always making
sure I did my homework first—S.W.

For Jan—D.O'C.

OXFORD
UNIVERSITY PRESS

Great Clarendon Street, Oxford OX2 6DP

Oxford University Press is a department of the University of Oxford.
It furthers the University's objective of excellence in research, scholarship,
and education by publishing worldwide. Oxford is a registered trade mark of
Oxford University Press in the UK and in certain other countries

Text copyright © Sam Watkins 2015
Illustrations copyright © David O'Connell 2015

The moral rights of the author and artist have been asserted

Database right Oxford University Press (maker)

First published 2015

British Library Cataloguing in Publication Data available

Data available

ISBN: 978-0-19-274267-4 (paperback)
ISBN: 978-0-19-274268-1 (eBook)

2 4 6 8 10 9 7 5 3 1

Printed in Great Britain

Paper used in the production of this book is a natural,
recyclable product made from wood grown in sustainable forests.
The manufacturing process conforms to the environmental
regulations of the country of origin.

CREATURE
TEACHER
GOES WILD

SAM WATKINS and
ILLUSTRATED BY David O'Connell

OXFORD
UNIVERSITY PRESS

CHAPTER 1:

WACKY WILF'S WILD ADVENTURE PARK

Zap! Zap! 'Eurrrrrgh.' Zap! Zap! 'Eurrrrrgh.' Zap-zap...

'Move your head, Barnaby!' Jake said. 'I want to see out the window.'

'No can do. These zombies won't zap themselves,' Barnaby replied, his eyes glued to his phone.

Sighing, Jake left Barnaby to his zombiezapping and looked down the coach. His teacher, Mr Hyde was at the back, wearing a purple pinstriped suit and strumming a ukulele.

'Okay, Year Fives,' he bellowed. 'One, two, three!

If you're happy that you're going to Wacky Wilf's Wild Adventure Park, clap your hands! If you're happy that you're going to Wacky Wilf's Wild Adventure Park, recite the alphabet backwards . . .'

Jake shook his head. 'Mr Hyde really is the craziest, funniest and best teacher in the world,' he murmured out loud.

'Solar System,' Nora corrected from her seat across the aisle.

'Universe!' added Woodstock, who was

sitting next to her.

They all grinned at each other. Mr Hyde *was* a great teacher. He made lessons fun. And he didn't make his class clean the toilets with their toothbrushes, like some teachers they'd had.

'I just hope he doesn't get *too* excited,' Nora whispered. 'You know how much he likes singing.'

Woodstock looked nervous. 'He could turn into Creature!'

Alexis' and Karl's heads popped up over the seat behind Nora and Woodstock.

'What was that about Creature?' Alexis asked.

'Nora thinks Mr Hyde might change into Creature if he gets too excited,' Jake explained.

'He does look pretty excited.' Karl pointed back at the loudly singing Mr Hyde. Jake was alarmed to see that his teacher's ears were looking extremely pink!

'You're right,' said Jake. 'Maybe one of us should sit near him.'

'I'll go and keep an eye on him,' Alexis said. 'Coming, Karl?'

She and Karl made their way to the back of the coach. The singing soon spread down the coach. Jake and Woodstock joined in—it was hard not to when Mr Hyde was around!

Nora hummed along, her nose in a leaflet. Suddenly she gasped.

'Guys, listen to this!' She read aloud:

'The adventure park and all the rides were designed by eccentric billionaire Wilfred Waldo Wellington Jr.'

'Wow. A *billion*aire!' Jake said.

Nora carried on. 'Mr Wellington prefers to be called Wilf—'

'*Class 5b pupils!* It is rude to gossip!'

They looked up. Mrs Blunt, the Headteacher, was swaying in the aisle on dangerously high heels, glaring at them.

Jake tried to look invisible but it was surprisingly difficult. Yesterday Mrs Blunt had given him two Sad Faces: the first for fidgeting in assembly, the second for groaning when she gave him the first. One more Sad Face and he'd have to work on the Rockery tomorrow, hauling horribly heavy rocks.

'Jake Jones—' Mrs Blunt started to speak, but the singing drowned her out.

'IF YOU'RE HAPPY AND YOU KNOW IT . . .'

The Headteacher stalked further down the aisle and clapped her hands sharply. The singing died away.

'And you reeeeeeeeallly want to show it . . .' sang Mr Hyde, with gusto, eyes closed, on his own. He had not seen Mrs Blunt.

'MIS-TER HYDE!'

The ukulele squeaked and fell silent.

'Attention, everyone,' the Head barked. 'It's very generous of Mr Wilfred Waldo Wellington Jr. to invite Classes 5a and 5b to the Opening Day of his brand new Adventure Park.

Mr Wellington is a Very Important Person. If he's impressed with you, he may contribute some money towards the headteacher statues I'm having placed in the school entrance. So I want you all on your best behaviour.'

She gave Mr Hyde a look. 'That goes for you too, Mr Hyde. No experimental teaching today. No horseplay, monkey business or tomfoolery. Understand?'

'No, Mrs Blunt. Um, I mean yes, Mrs Blunt,' Mr Hyde said.

'Hmph. We'll see.'

Mrs Blunt stomped back to the front of the coach through an uneasy silence. But Mr Hyde was too excited to stay quiet for long.

'Hey, who knows this one? Aga-doo, doo, doo, push pineapple, shake the tree ...'

Jake started to join in, but then stopped. Woodstock's face had gone red and he looked about to explode.

'What's up with Woodstock?' Jake whispered to Nora.

'Mrs Blunt promised funding for a new art studio,' Nora whispered back. 'The old one is falling to pieces. Woodstock and some other pupils have been raising money for it—'

'But now she says she's putting all the money towards statues of all the school's headteachers. Says they're for "posterity", whatever that means!' Woodstock fumed.

'It's just a way of getting a statue of herself,' Nora muttered.

Jake was shocked. 'She can't do that!'

'She can, she's the Head,' Woodstock said, staring out of the window from beneath his long fringe. 'It's totally uncool. But I don't want to talk about it.'

Nora tried to cheer him up. She pointed to the adventure park leaflet.

'Woodstock, there are crocodiles in the Wildlife Zone,' she said. 'I can speak crocodile, you know. Aə-ə-r-r-r-rahhhh əh əhhhh.'

Barnaby looked up and sniggered. 'How rude. You can't say that.'

Nora glared at him. 'That was actually crocodile for "Nice to meet you".'

'Nice to *eat* you, more like!' Jake joked.

Woodstock almost smiled.

Nora went red. 'It's true! I've researched it. Crocodiles talk in grunts and croaks. And sometimes they even roar. Like this—'

'HURRRRAAAAAAAAAAHHHHH!'

A cheer had erupted at the back of the coach.

'LOOK! A sign for Wilfy Wildo's Wacky Whatsit Park!' Mr Hyde said.

Jake turned. His teacher was bouncing up and down and pointing excitedly out of the window.

'We're nearly there! Oh I can't *wait* to go on Ziggy's Zip Wire and the Rushing Rocky Rapids and the Wild West Zone looks cool but I'm not going on the Ghost Train and the rollercoaster looks mega-scary . . . and . . . and . . . ' Mr Hyde jumped to his feet and burst into song.

'AGA-DOO . . . DOO . . . OOOOH!

There's another sign, we'll be there in two shakes of a kipper . . . kipperrr . . . '

An alarm bell rang in Jake's head.

Mr Hyde had gone very red . . .

Too red! His ears weren't pink any more—they were starting to glow!

Alexis and Karl were too busy looking out of the window to notice.

'What's that burning rubber smell?' said Nora, sniffing.

Jake leapt to his feet. *Mr Hyde was changing into Creature!*

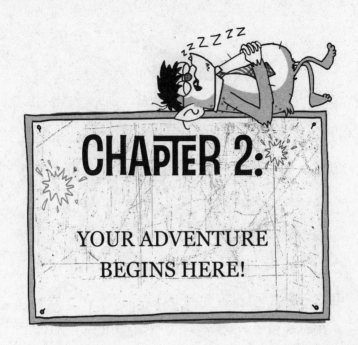

CHAPTER 2:

YOUR ADVENTURE BEGINS HERE!

'*Mr Hyde!*'

Jake raced up the aisle, grabbing a sick bag he spotted on the way. Karl and Alexis were trying to get the glowing Mr Hyde to sit down.

'Here—' Jake thrust the bag over his teacher's face.

'Breathe deeply, sir.'

Mr Hyde breathed deeply and pulled a face.

'Ugh!' he said. 'Why are you making me sniff
tuna sandwiches, Jake?!'

'That's my lunch!' A Class 5a boy shoved Jake
aside and grabbed the bag.

Jake put his hands up. 'Sorry . . . '

Karl and Alexis pulled Mr Hyde back into his seat just as Nora and Woodstock appeared.

'Is he okay?' Nora asked.

They all looked at Mr Hyde. He looked a bit pink, but he wasn't glowing anymore.

'What was that bag thing about?' Mr Hyde questioned.

'Sir, you were *glowing!*' Nora whispered.

'Glowing? Thank you, Nora. It's my new skin care regime . . . Oh, I see. You thought I was changing! Don't worry, I've got this Creature thing under control . . . *Holy kipper, we're HERE!*'

The cry went up. 'WE'RE HERE!!'

Jake raced back down the coach to his seat, elbowed Barnaby out of the way and pressed his nose to the window.

'Hey!' Barnaby protested. 'You made me miss the Head Zombie!'

Jake pointed out of the window. 'Forget zombies, Barnaby—we've arrived!'

As the coach rolled to a stop, Mrs Blunt stood up, but was steam-rollered back down under a tide of shrieking pupils.

'SIT DOWN EVERYONE! Oliver Smith, a Sad Face for pushing. And one for you, Maisy Maxwell . . .'

Hiiiisssssssss! The coach doors opened and Jake and his friends spilled into the car park. He stopped and gazed around. In front of him towered a building of gleaming metal and glass. It looked like a humungous space port. Across the front was a huge, glowing sign.

'WACKY WILF'S WILD ADVENTURE PARK.'

'Wooo . . . ' he breathed.

'Wooow . . . ' breathed fifty-one other awestruck pupils.

'Wowsers!' Mr Hyde exclaimed. He turned to Miss Trimble, Class 5a's nervy teacher. 'Looks cool, doesn't it, Miss Trimble?'

Miss Trimble hesitated. 'It looks . . . clean,' she said, finally.

Mrs Blunt marched everyone into the Space Port building and across a spotless silver floor to a desk. A sign above it read:

YOUR ADVENTURE
BEGINS HERE!

A man in a
spacesuit came
round stamping
everyone's hands.

'QUIET!' Mrs Blunt
bellowed.

The chatter faded.

'You will be placed in groups.
You will stay with your group
all day. No one is to go off on
their own, unless they wish
to do time on the Rockery.
Each group will consist of
six pupils and one Responsible
Adult. Read out the groups, Miss
Trimble.'

Miss Trimble shuffled forward.

'Group 1. Nora Newton, Karl McQueen, Woodstock Stone . . .'

Jake crossed his fingers. *Please let me be with my friends . . .*

'Alexis Williams, Barnaby McCrumb . . . and Jake Jones. Responsible Adult: Mr Hyde.'

Jake high-fived Karl and Woodstock. They looked round for Mr Hyde, but he was nowhere to be seen.

A surge of cold fear went through Jake. *Surely he hasn't changed . . . has he?* He looked at the others. 'We have to find Mr Hyde, quick!'

'Don't panic—there he is,' Karl said, pointing.

Mr Hyde was bounding towards them, waving a large piece of paper.

'Sir, please don't go off on your own—' Nora began.

'From now on I will stick to you like chewing gum on your shoe,' Mr Hyde said. 'Okay, are we ready for adventures?! I've got a map . . . '

They all crowded round.

Mr Hyde scratched his head. 'Hmmm. I can't quite . . . what's this big pink blob?'

'A whale?' Karl suggested.

Nora shook her head. 'An ice cream.'

There was another bark from Mrs Blunt.

'One final thing. I want everyone back here at one o'clock on the dot for the Grand Opening Ceremony. I will do a head count at that time. If anyone is missing, or is even half a millisecond late, there will be Trouble with a capital "R". Do I make myself clear?'

A sea of blank, uncomprehending faces gazed at the Head.

'Oh, I get it!' Nora exclaimed. 'R is for "Rockery",' she called.

'One person remembered their brain this morning,' snapped Mrs Blunt. 'Right, everyone, you may go. Oh, before your group leaves, Miss Trimble, I want a word with you and Amelia.'

As the groups began to head off, Jake heard a loud, bossy voice.

'MAKE WAY! Mrs Blunt wants to speak to me!'

Jake looked round. A girl with scraped-back blonde hair was barging through the crowd. Amelia Trotter-Hogg, Most Annoying Person in the Universe. Jake saw her elbow Nora in the back as she walked past their group. Nora yelped.

'Whoops, didn't see you there, Boring Nora,' Amelia sniggered.

'Say sorry, Amelia,' Jake said, gritting his teeth.

'Flaky Jake sticking up for Boring Nora—how *sweet*.' She flounced off.

Jake felt rage building up in his stomach. He started to go after her but Nora grabbed his arm and held him back.

'Don't, Jake. You'll get in trouble.'

Jake reluctantly turned back to the others, who were still trying to work out the map.

'Where shall we go first?' Alexis asked.

Mr Hyde peered at the map. 'How about the Alien Zone? There, look. A picture of an alien . . . '

Jake tried to listen, but he was still fuming about Amelia. He looked over to where Amelia, Mrs Blunt and Miss Trimble had their heads together. As he watched, all three of them looked up and seemed to stare directly at him and his group! He flushed, and looked away quickly. *Why are they looking over? Is Amelia trying to get Class 5b pupils in trouble?*

'Come on, Jake!' called Mr Hyde.

His group were moving off. He cast another glance at Amelia. She held his gaze for a few seconds, smirking nastily.

'JAKE!!'

He ran to catch up with others. *It isn't only Mr Hyde I'll need to keep an eye on today,* he thought.

CHAPTER 3:

THE FLOWER POWER FAIRY ZONE

'Are we nearly there yet?' Woodstock asked. 'My feet hurt.'

Jake and his group had been walking for a quarter of an hour and still had not found the Alien Zone. That would have been bad enough, but ever since leaving the entrance, Amelia's group had been trailing along just behind them. Jake could hear her irritating snigger almost constantly.

'They must be going to the Alien Zone, too,' Nora whispered to Jake.

'Yeah . . . maybe.' Jake thought about the secretive conversation between Amelia, Mrs Blunt and Miss Trimble at the entrance. *Was it coincidence that Amelia's group was going exactly the same way as them? Or was there something—*

'Ooof! Sorry . . . '

He had bumped into Mr Hyde, who had screeched to a halt just in front of him.

'That's odd,' Mr Hyde said, squinting at a sign over the path.

THE FLOWER POWER FAIRY ZONE

Jake and his friends all looked at each other.

'There's no way I'm going in there,' Barnaby snorted. 'You promised me aliens.'

Barnaby had a point. The Flower Power Fairies were characters in a little kid's show. At the end of each episode they shouted '*Peace and Love!*' Jake's sister, Connie, loved it, but she was only three. Jake hated it.

Mr Hyde looked at the map, puzzled.

'But there are pictures of aliens . . . '

Nora took the map. 'They're not aliens, they're flowers!'

'PEACE AND LOVE!' Amelia shouted.

Jake winced. Amelia's group had arrived. She looked at the Flower Power Fairy Zone sign, then smirked at Barnaby.

'Big rides too scary for you, McCrumb?'

Barnaby glared at her. 'Following us around again, Hogg-Trotter?'

'IT'S TROTTER-HOGG!!' Amelia snarled.

'Calm down, everyone,' Mr Hyde soothed as Miss Trimble bustled up. 'We were looking for the Alien Zone, but somehow we've got lost.'

'Oh yes Mr Hyde, the map is very confusing, isn't it?' Miss Trimble said. 'But this zone looks nice . . . '

Nora was still looking at the map. 'I *think* we can go through here to the Alien Zone.'

'Fantabulous! Off we go, then!' Mr Hyde exclaimed. Ignoring Barnaby's grumbling, he marched under the sign, followed by Jake and his friends.

Jake blinked as a rainbow of colours hit his eyes. Everywhere, monstrous, brightly painted flowers sprouted, as tall as trees. Fountains of coloured water sprang up as they walked past, with shimmering rainbows hovering around them. Miniature carousels revolved slowly to tinkling music. Smiley people dressed in flower costumes wandered around.

'Peace and Love!' sang a daisy to Barnaby.

Barnaby scowled. 'Whatever.'

As they made their way across the Flower Power Fairy Zone, Jake could still hear Amelia's voice just behind them. His stomach tightened. *I won't let Amelia ruin our day!*

He made a decision. 'Let's lose Amelia,' he muttered to the others. 'She's up to something.'

They nodded in agreement.

Jake started to walk faster. So did Woodstock, Nora, Alexis and Karl.

'That's the spirit!' Mr Hyde said, striding along. 'A nice brisk pace.'

But it was no good. The faster they walked, the faster Amelia's group followed. Jake felt crosser and crosser. And Barnaby wasn't helping—he was slowing them down, his eyes still glued to his zombie game. As they dashed past a carousel, Jake looked over his shoulder. Amelia's group had fallen behind and Amelia seemed to be arguing with Miss Trimble.

Suddenly, off to one side, Jake saw a little flower-covered archway.

'Quick—in there!' he said to the others. With any luck, Amelia wouldn't see where they went.

One by one, they ducked under the arch. Inside, a lady dressed as a daffodil fairy was sitting on a toadstool, pouring glitter into pots.

She looked up.

'Peace and love!'

'Peace and love to you too,' Mr Hyde said, politely.

zap zap! Barnaby wandered through the arch, still busy destroying zombies. *zap, zap, aargh . . .*

TAN-TARA!

TAN-TARA!

TAN-TARA!

Barnaby nearly dropped his phone in fright as trumpets started to toot and bells started to sound all around them!

The daffodil jumped off her toadstool.

'You're the Lucky Thirteenth visitor to the Flower Power Bower!' she cried, prancing merrily towards Barnaby with a pair of silver wings and a pot of fairy dust. 'You've won a pair of wings, dear!'

'Aaaargh—get off!' Barnaby squawked, pushing the wings away. But the daffodil was not put off that easily.

'Some fairy dust, then?' she cried. She tipped the pot of fairy dust over Barnaby's head.

Barnaby's face turned an angry shade of glittery red. The fairy looked less happy.

'You're not . . . allergic to glitter, are you?' she asked, nervously.

There was a cackle of horrid laughter from behind them.

Jake closed his eyes. *Great. Just what we need.* Amelia was standing in the archway, her group at her side.

ook, it's Sparkly McCrumb, the Biscuit
!' Amelia giggled.

Barnaby looked as if he might explode.

'THAT'S IT!' he shouted. 'I've had enough
of this!'

He pushed his way past Amelia and her
group and stormed out of the Flower Power
Bower.

'Barnaby!' Jake called.

But Mr Hyde stopped him. 'Give him
a second to cool off outside.'

Amelia looked at the daffodil fairy.

'Hey, if he doesn't want the wings, can
I have them?' asked Amelia.

The daffodil looked uncertain.

'Well, I'm not supposed to—'

'Oh go on . . . ' Amelia grabbed the wings.

The daffodil tried to hold on to them, but Amelia wrestled them out of her grasp. The daffodil gave up—she knew when she'd been beaten. 'Well, all right,' she sighed. 'Just don't tell anyone! Now, I need a photo for the Hall of Fairy Fame . . . wait there while I get the camera . . .'

'Let's go and meet Barnaby,' Mr Hyde said to Jake and his classmates as Amelia grabbed a mirror from her bag and started smoothing down hairs that didn't need smoothing.

They all ducked through the archway.

'This,' said Woodstock, 'is officially becoming a nightmare.'

Karl laughed. 'Barnaby would agree with you.'

Jake looked round. 'Hang on,' he said. 'Where is he?'

Barnaby had vanished!

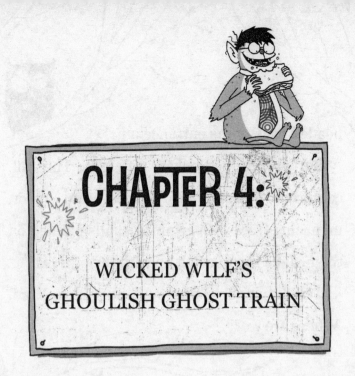

CHAPTER 4:

WICKED WILF'S
GHOULISH GHOST TRAIN

'BARNABYYYYYYY!' shouted Jake.

They walked all round the Flower Power Fairy Zone calling for Barnaby, but he didn't appear. Finally, Mr Hyde stopped them.

'We'll have to go back and report him missing,' he said.

Jake groaned. *All that way, for nothing!* He trudged gloomily after the others, as they headed back to the entrance.

But everything looked different. The tall, colourful flowers had turned into taller, menacing trees with grinning skulls painted on them. Jake ran to catch up with the others.

'We didn't come this way,' he said to Nora. 'Where are we?'

Nora looked at the map. 'It's not clear, but I think we're in Spookyville . . . '

Suddenly, Karl gave a shout. 'There's Barnaby!'

Way ahead, on the path, Jake saw the unmistakeable figure of his classmate. Barnaby stared at them for a moment. Then he started running.

'BARNABYYYYYYY!' yelled Mr Hyde and tore off after him. As Jake tried to keep up, he saw first Barnaby, and then Mr Hyde, swerve off the path. By the time Jake and the others reached the end of the path, both had disappeared.

'Where'd they go?' panted Nora.

'In there, maybe?' Karl pointed to a black building. Splattered across the front in dripping red letters were the words:

WICKED WILF'S
GHOULISH GHOST TRAIN

They raced into the building and through a turnstile into a dark corridor. Ahead, Jake could see Mr Hyde at the back of a queue of people, craning to peer over the sea of heads. They ran to join him.

'Is he there, sir?' Jake asked.

'I think he jumped the queue,' Mr Hyde said. 'But it's too dark to see . . . what is this place?'

'The ghost train, sir.'

Mr Hyde's face drained of colour. For a minute, Jake thought he was going to turn back. But a steely look came into his eye.

'You're a Responsible Adult, Hydey,' Mr Hyde muttered to himself. 'There's a lost student in there—probably terrified out of his wits—and it's your duty to find him!'

They reached the front of the queue as an empty train rattled up. Jake saw that it consisted of three small carriages. Karl and Woodstock got in the first, Nora and Alexis in the second. Jake and a very pale-looking Mr Hyde slid into the last carriage. The train started moving.

'We're not going to spend all day chasing Barnaby, are we?' Alexis grumbled, as they chugged towards a curtain.

'Barnaby's upset,' Mr Hyde said. 'He's your friend, and I'm a firm believer in friends sticking together.'

Alexis pulled a face. 'He didn't stick with us!'

'Friends stick together . . .' Mr Hyde repeated, as the train plunged into a dark tunnel.

' . . . Together . . . together . . . together . . . ' came an echo.

Everyone jumped. Mr Hyde yelped, and pulled his jacket over his head. Then, with a rattle, a plastic skeleton swung out of the wall towards them.

Karl and Woodstock burst out laughing. 'Scary—not!' said Karl.

Nora snorted. 'That skeleton is wrong—

46

there are actually 206 bones in a human
skeleton.'

'Trust you to spot that!' Jake grinned.

After a few more anatomically incorrect
skeletons had popped out of the walls, the train
emerged into what looked like a dimly lit dining
hall. A grandfather clock ticked loudly in a
corner.

With a groan, the train shuddered to a halt.

'Why have we stopped?' Mr Hyde yelped,
peeking out from under his coat.

'I don't know,' Jake said, puzzled.

DONG!!!

The deafening sound shattered the silence.
The grandfather clock was chiming!

Jake clapped his hands over his ears as the
racket continued.

DONG! DONG! DONG!!!

It chimed twelve times. As the twelfth dong died dismally away, ghoulish figures emerged from the shadows.

'Nnnnneeeuuuuuurrrrrghhh . . . ' moaned the figures.

'*Zombies!*' Woodstock shouted.

The zombies lurched towards the train with jerky, mechanical movements. Jake realized they must be models. *They look pretty realistic, though,* he thought! They stopped an arm's length from the train and stood flailing and moaning.

'Euuuurrrrrghhhh!' moaned the nearest zombie to Jake, waving a gruesome, bloody arm.

Jake laughed. 'Euuuurrrghhhh to you too! I wonder what it's made of . . . '

He grabbed the zombie's arm and squeezed it, hard.

RRRRRRRRRIPPPPPP! The arm came off in his hand.

'Aaargh—my arm!' the zombie groaned, staggering back.

Jake felt an icy shock zap through his veins.

'IT'S REAL!' Nora shrieked. Everyone gasped.

The zombie lurched towards Jake again.

'You have angered the Head Zombie!'

the zombie howled. 'Now he will eat your braaaaaaaaaaaaiiiins . . . '

Mr Hyde shot back under his coat. Heart racing, Jake brandished the arm he was still clutching. It was some kind of hard plastic—good for a weapon . . .

Plastic . . . his brain whirred. Then it clicked. *Plastic?! Of course it's plastic, you nitwit—zombies aren't real . . .*

'Whack it!' Karl shouted. 'Destroy the zombie.'

A light bulb went on in Jake's brain. He knew someone else who liked to destroy zombies. He lowered the arm.

'Take that mask off, Barnaby,' said Jake. 'I know it's you.'

Nora gasped. '*Barnaby?!*'

The Head Zombie laughed and took his mask off.

'Ha ha. Had you fooled for a minute, didn't I?!' Barnaby was smirking.

'You'll get us all in trouble, Barnaby,' said Nora angrily.

Barnaby shrugged. 'Yeah, yeah. It was funny, though . . . '

Jake whirled round to speak to Mr Hyde.

'We've found him . . . Sir?'

Mr Hyde had retreated completely inside his coat. Almost like he'd shrunk.

'Mr Hyde!' said Jake, tugging his sleeve. 'OWWWW!'

Jake jerked his hand back. The coat was red hot! A strange glow came from beneath it. Sucking his burnt fingers, Jake realized what was happening.

'Quick, tap your leg, sir!' he cried. Mr Hyde

could sometimes stop himself changing by tapping his leg.

But it was too late.

All six pupils stared open-mouthed as orange rays of light began to stream from the buttonholes and sleeves of the coat. Smoke poured from the neck, and Jake could smell burning rubber.

Nora leapt to her feet. 'Noooooooooooo . . .'

Barnaby dived for cover under the dining table.

'JAKE! GET OUT!' shouted Alexis.

Jake leapt over into Alexis and Nora's carriage and ducked down . . .

FAAAAAAAAAAAAAARRRRRT!

Wheeeeeeee . . . .

POP! POP! POP!

BANG!

CHAPTER 5:

WONKY WILF'S MAD MIRROR MAZE

Mr Hyde's coat burst like an over-inflated purple balloon as the fart filled it. A rain of purple fabric fluttered down on Jake and his classmates' heads.

Silence.

Even the mechanical zombies had stopped groaning. Jake, Nora and Alexis slowly lifted their heads and stared at each other.

No one moved.

'What's happening?' Jake heard Karl whisper from the front car.

'Has he . . . changed?' Woodstock whispered.

Very carefully, Jake pulled himself up and peered into the last carriage. As the cloud of smoke cleared, he saw a small, hairy creature squatting on the seat where Mr Hyde's coat had been moments before. It squinted at Jake through black-rimmed glasses.

Mr Hyde's glasses.

Jake swallowed. The worst had happened. Mr Hyde had changed into Creature! Jake reached behind him.

'Someone give me a bag, quick . . . '

If he could just . . . he felt a bag pushed into his hand. He slowly held it out over Creature, who was nibbling experimentally on the plastic zombie arm.

'Niiiiice Creature,' whispered Jake, leaning over . . .

'YIK!' Creature threw the arm away. It whacked Jake on the head.

'OW!' Jake lost his balance and toppled into the back carriage. He tried to grab the startled Creature as he fell, but missed.

'Kippppppppeeeeeeerrrrrrrrrrrrr!' Creature bounded off the train. Straight into Barnaby, who was crawling out from under the table.

Barnaby squawked. 'Gerroff!'

Creature grabbed Barnaby's ears and swung himself up onto his head.

'YOOOWWWW!' howled Barnaby.

Every one of Creature's hairs stood on end. He shot off Barnaby's head like a rocket-propelled hedgehog and landed on a huge chandelier that was hanging right above the train. The chandelier lurched dangerously. Creature chattered crossly at Barnaby.

'My ears have stretched!' Barnaby groaned, rubbing them.

'It's your own fault!' Nora exclaimed. 'You made him change . . . '

Barnaby shrugged. 'Blah blah—'

Creeeeeeeeeeeeeeeeeaokkkkkkkk . . .

'...blah...' Barnaby's voice trailed away. He stared up at the swaying chandelier.

'What's that?' Nora rubbed her eyes. Jake coughed. Bits of plaster were falling on his head. He looked back up, and sucked his breath in sharply.

Creature's weight was too much for the chandelier. Slowly but surely, it was ripping out of the ceiling.

'It's coming down!' Alexis screamed.

Jake jumped up. 'Off the train!' he yelled, but was thrown back in his seat as the train suddenly jerked forwards!

Creeeeeeeeeeakkkk . . .

With a squawk, Creature somersaulted off the chandelier.

CRAAAAASH!!

A mangled mess of metal landed in a shower of plaster on the track behind the moving train, missing Jake by millimetres. As the train lurched into a tunnel, Jake caught a glimpse of Creature disappearing through a side door, followed by Barnaby.

Then they were plunged into darkness.

For what seemed an age, the train hurtled along in the dark. At last, it emerged into the light and juddered to a halt at the station.

Jake scrambled out, then stopped. 'This isn't where we got on!'

The platform was lined with mirrors. A voice

boomed through a speaker.

'Welcome to Wonky Wilf's Mad Mirror Maze! Can you find your way to the front entrance without losing your mind?!'

Jake turned to the others. 'We've got to catch Creature,' he said.

'And Barnaby,' Nora reminded him. 'I saw them both go through a side door.'

Jake nodded. 'We need to find them before the Opening Ceremony!'

'But how?' Woodstock asked.

'That announcement just said there was another entrance. We'll go through the maze and get out that way and start to look,' Karl said.

They ran along the platform to a door. Jake pushed it open and stepped through.

'Whoa . . . '

He was in a room full of hundreds—maybe thousands—of Jakes!

An army of Noras appeared behind the army of Jakes. Then hundreds of Karls and Woodstocks, and finally Jake saw Alexis reflected many times over. They were all oohing and ahhing. Every time Jake moved, his reflections moved too. It made him feel dizzy.

'Right,' said Jake, looking around. 'That way.'

He walked forward. **WHACK!** Straight into a mirror.

'This way!' called Nora. Jake tried to follow what he thought was Nora, but a mirror blocked his way. He'd been following her reflection!

'Jake! Where are you?' he heard Alexis call. He saw a flash of her red football shirt, then nothing. Karl and Woodstock, too, had vanished.

Don't panic, Jake sternly told his reflections. Suddenly there was a movement behind him! A dark shape flashed briefly into view in one of the mirrors, then vanished.

He whirled round. *Was that Creature?*

'Flawless, absolutely flawless.'

Someone was murmuring from around the corner! He peered round.

Amelia! Jake quickly whipped his head back. Miss Trimble was probably not far away, then. And if Creature *was* in here . . . Jake peered round the corner again.

Amelia was pouting at herself in a mirror. She bent down to fish around in her bag and brought out a pair of pink sunglasses.

Jake started to back away. But then he

stopped. The mirror Amelia had been looking
in was being slid to one side!

A furry face with glasses appeared.

Jake staggered backwards. *Creature!*

Amelia stood up, sunglasses on. She looked
in the mirror.

'Mwah!' She pouted.

'BUURRRRRRRRRRP!' Creature pouted back.

'ARGHHHHHHHHHHHHH!!!!'

Amelia screamed so loudly Jake thought every mirror in the maze would shatter! Creature cackled. Then he grabbed Amelia's sunglasses, and disappeared.

Amelia stared at the hole where Creature had vanished, and let out a howl.

'BARNABY MCCRUMB! I know that was you!!'

She charged off down a dark, twisty-turny corridor lined with all kinds of strange mirrors at odd angles. Jake followed at what he thought was a safe distance. But suddenly there was a Creaturish cackle behind him. Amelia heard it too, and whirled round.

Jake had no time to hide.

'Jake Jones!' Amelia cried. '*You* took my sunglasses?!'

Jake was about to deny this, when he saw Amelia's face go deathly white. She didn't say a word to Jake, just stared. She pointed a trembling finger.

'Behind you . . .'

Jake turned round, very slowly. His mouth dropped open.

In the darkness behind him stood a gigantic, menacing, hairy shape!

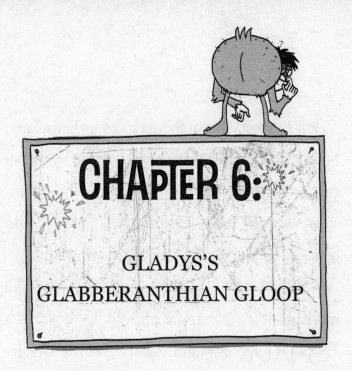

CHAPTER 6:

GLADYS'S GLABBERANTHIAN GLOOP

The monster opened its mouth in a yawn showing two rows of sharp, sharp teeth.

THUD. Amelia dropped to the floor in a dead faint.

Jake started to back away, then turned to flee. To his horror, two more enormous figures with stretched-out limbs and huge heads were approaching from the other side. He was trapped!

But . . . wait! One of these monsters had a long, floppy fringe. The other was wearing a white lab coat and glasses.

Woodstock and Nora! The mirrors had distorted then. So the other figure must be . . .

'CREATURE!' Jake pelted towards the monster—

SMACK! Straight into a mirror. As he clutched his throbbing nose, it struck him what was happening. He hadn't seen Creature—he'd seen Creature's *reflection* in a distorting mirror! Jake looked in the mirror next to him. He looked normal size. Then he took a few steps back. His reflection suddenly slid upwards till it was several metres tall. The further away you stood, the taller you got!

Nora and Woodstock screeched up beside him.

'Where's Creature?' Nora asked.

'It was only his reflection,' Jake said, exasperated.

At that moment, Alexis and Karl appeared. Karl had a large bruise on his forehead.

'That just happened to us, too!' Alexis explained. 'Karl ran headfirst into a mirror!'

She suddenly spotted Amelia, still out cold on the floor.

'Amelia! What happened?'

'She fainted. We'll have to get her out of here,' Jake said.

They prodded Amelia until she opened her eyes.

'W-where's the monster?' she burbled, looking around blearily.

'It wasn't a monster,' Jake said. 'It was . . . um

. . . just your reflection. Come on.'

Jake and Woodstock pulled Amelia along mirrored corridors till they finally found the front entrance. As they went out, Jake saw a figure slouching against the wall looking bored.

It was Barnaby, wearing pink sunglasses!

Amelia went as pink as the sunglasses. She marched up to him and grabbed them.

'I knew it was you who stole them!'

'I didn't steal them, I found them,' Barnaby protested. 'On the floor in the maze.'

'Liar—'

'AMELIA!'

Amelia was interrupted

by a shout. Miss Trimble was flapping towards them, the rest of her group trailing after her.

'You shouldn't have run off, Amelia,' she panted. 'You know what Mrs Blunt said!'

Amelia suddenly threw Jake a sly look.

'Yes—teachers must stay with their groups! So where's YOUR teacher, Jake Jones?'

'He went . . . to the loo,' Jake said.

'I don't believe you. He's doing something off curriculum again! Mrs Blunt said—'

'Mrs Blunt *told* you to keep an eye on Mr Hyde, didn't she?' Jake exclaimed. 'That's why you've been following us.'

Miss Trimble wrung her hands. 'Children, let's not argue . . . '

Amelia ignored her. 'I'm phoning Mrs Blunt. She gave me her mobile number in case something like this happened . . . ' She reached for her bag.

Her face dropped.

'My bag! I've left it somewhere in the mirror place!'

'Oh dear.' Miss Trimble tutted. 'Mr Hyde's group, wait here. My group, follow me. We will find Amelia's bag together.'

As Amelia's group trooped back into the maze, Jake turned to the others.

'I knew it—Mrs Blunt told Amelia to spy on Mr Hyde!'

Nora looked worried. 'And now she's gone back into the maze—and Creature's in there . . . '

Barnaby jumped up. 'No he's not . . . ' He pointed.

In the distance, Jake saw a brown ball of fur bouncing across the grass towards a huge orange dome that looked like a half-sunken Saturn, a giant ring swooping round it at an angle.

House-sized letters on the ring read:

ALIEN ZONE

'After him!' Jake shouted.

They raced off after Creature. As they neared the dome it got busier and busier—everyone seemed to be going to the Alien Zone! By the time they had pushed through the crowds Creature had disappeared.

As they reached the entrance, Jake heard a distant shout.

'HEY!'

They turned, to see Amelia and her group galloping after them.

'Why can't that pony-tailed pest leave us alone?' Karl grumbled.

'She wants an excuse to phone Mrs Blunt,' Alexis said. 'Let's go.'

They ran into the dome. It wasn't called the Alien Zone for nothing! Aliens of all shapes, sizes and colours milled about. Green goggle-eyed ones. Purple pimple-nosed ones. Furry, cute ones. Slimy, not-so cute ones. Small, annoying ones—Jake realized that a lot of little kids were dressed in alien costumes . . . there was a tug on his sleeve.

'Amelia's catching up!' Nora hissed.

Jake glanced back, and caught a glimpse of a blonde, pony-tailed head bobbing through the crowd.

'We'll have to hide!' he said.

'But where?' Karl asked.

They all looked around frantically. A few metres away, Jake spotted a little food stall.

A handwritten sign on the counter said 'Back in 5 mins. Gladys'.

Jake pointed. 'There.'

They dashed behind the stall. Barnaby dipped his finger in the huge vat of slimy green stuff on the counter.

'Mmm—like lime jelly, only gloopier—'

'Barnaby, GET DOWN!'

Karl and Alexis yanked Barnaby down just as Amelia burst out of the crowd and screeched to a halt a few metres away.

Everyone held their breath. Jake heard Miss Trimble's voice.

'Are you *sure* they came this way, Amelia?'

'I saw them! Oh Miss, can I phone Mrs Blunt now?'

Suddenly a shadow fell over Jake. With a sinking feeling, he looked up. A large lady in a green alien costume was standing over him, her antennae twitching angrily.

Gladys! Jake realized in dismay.

'Honestly, I leave my stall for five minutes, only to find it's been infested with CHILDREN!' Gladys growled. 'Out! All of you. This is not a place for hide-and-seek!'

Red-faced, Jake slowly started to get to his feet. Nora did too.

'Come along, I've got customers to serve!' Gladys leaned over to speak to someone on the other side of the stall. 'Won't be a minute, little fellow . . . hey—what are you doing?! STOP!!'

SPLOOOOOOOSH!!!!

Jake threw himself back down as green gloop sprayed everywhere. Gladys's "customer" had jumped into the vat of Glabberanthian Gloop!

CHAPTER 7:

ZIGGY'S ZIP WIRE

The huge vat of gloop teetered one way . . .
then the other . . .

It came to rest with a rattle.

Gladys's mouth fell open. Jake stared up at the vat. Slowly, a glistening green head emerged over the rim.

'Hic!'

Jake's eyes nearly popped out.

CREATURE!

Gladys found her voice. 'My beautiful gloop!' She grabbed a large wooden spoon from the counter and advanced on Creature.

Jake leapt up, followed by the others.

'NO!' Nora shouted.

'Don't touch him!' Alexis cried, striking a karate pose.

'THERE THEY ARE!'

Jake groaned. In his eagerness to catch Creature, he'd forgotten Amelia! She marched towards the stall, phone in hand, followed by Miss Trimble.

'No more children over here.' Gladys waved the spoon menacingly. 'I'm closed.'

Amelia waved her phone belligerently. 'Well you can't stop me.' She continued to stomp forward.

Miss Trimble fluttered like a confused chicken.

'We're trapped!' gasped Nora.

A rattle made Jake look round. Creature was hauling himself out of the gloop. The vat was starting to lean over . . . further and further . . .

KEERRR-RAAAASH!

. . . he tumbled to the ground in front of the stall.

SPLOOOSH!!!!

Amelia gave a scream that turned into a gurgle as a wave of green gloop knocked her off her feet. With a wet-sounding squelch, Creature hurtled off into the crowd.

'Nooooooo . . .' wailed Gladys, sinking to her knees.

Jake shouted to the others.

'Run!'

They bolted out from behind the stall, past the gibbering Gladys, and sprinted after Creature. Although he had disappeared into the crowd, it was easy to see where he'd gone from the sticky trail of green gloop. The trail led into another domed building.

Jake read the sign.

ZIGGY'S
ZIP WIRE

Karl groaned. 'Creature on a zip wire? Sounds like trouble!'

Barnaby smirked. 'Sounds like fun!'

At that moment a loud voice broke across the noise of the crowd.

'Slow down, Amelia! Monsters? Green gloop? You're cracking up . . .'

'It's Mrs Blunt! In here, NOW!' Jake hissed.

They scurried into Ziggy's Zip Wire dome.

Jake peeked back out. He saw Mrs Blunt bulldozing through the crowd, phone pressed to her ear. She stopped in front of the zip wire building, just as a gloopy, wild-eyed Amelia appeared.

'They're bound to come in here,' he heard Woodstock whisper. 'We'll have to go up to the zip wire!'

They ran to the lift, but there was a very long queue.

'We can't wait,' said Nora in a panicky voice. 'Oh—look!'

She pointed to a trail of green footprints on the floor. They followed it to a small door.

DO YOU DARE TAKE THE STAIR?

'Do You Dare Take The Stair?' a sign above it asked.

Jake opened the door.

'We dare!' he said, and began to climb.

Ten minutes later, Jake didn't feel so daring. It was the longest, wobbliest staircase ever, and creaked horribly at every step. Finally they reached a metal platform. It swayed as they stepped onto it, making Jake's stomach lurch.

'Eurrgh,' said Nora, closing her eyes. 'How high are we?'

'I've been higher,' muttered Barnaby, staring hard at his shoes.

'Where's Creature?' Alexis asked.

Jake looked around. From the far side of the platform two thick wires snaked across the dome. In front of them stood a queue of children, some wearing alien costumes. As Jake watched, two kids in costumes were being strapped into chairs hanging from the wires. One of them was wriggling around a lot, to the annoyance of the alien-suited man trying to strap him in.

Wait—there's something weird about that kid . . . Jake looked closer.

He was wearing thick glasses. And he looked green, furry and . . . *gloopy?!*

'Creature! He's going on the zip wire!' cried Jake.

Nora gasped. 'We've got to stop him!'

Ignoring angry mutters from the crowd, they started to push their way to the front of the queue. Jake saw the zip wire man grab a lever.

'STOP!' he yelled.

Too late.

'KIPPPPPPPPPPPPPPPPPPPP PPPPPERRRRRRRRRRRRRR!'

Creature screamed, as he shot off down the wire at top speed, gloopy green fur flying out behind him.

Jake ran up to the zip wire man.

'Excuse me . . . '

The man put his hand up. 'No queue jumping!' he said, sternly. 'Who's next?'

Nora broke in. 'Please—one of those kids who

just went down—is my little brother, we've got to go after him! He just ran off . . . '

The man looked alarmed. 'Oh dear! Well, I suppose you'd better go next, then. You'll have to go two at a time.'

There was grumbling from the crowd.

'Barnaby, we'll go first,' said Jake. Barnaby didn't look happy about this, but Alexis pushed him forward. 'You've been higher,' she reminded him, grinning.

The man strapped them in.

'Ready?' he asked. Jake gulped and nodded. Barnaby shut his eyes tightly.

'Here goes . . . '

The lever was pulled. Jake felt his chair jerk forward, then with a surge of adrenalin, he slid out into dizzying space, slowly at first but getting faster and faster, till he could hardly catch his breath. Crowds of ant-like people scurried below him, and he sailed above the highest loop of the rollercoaster, just as a car full of screaming people hurtled over the top!

'Woooooo-hoooooooo!' he yelled to Barnaby on the other wire.

Barnaby didn't woo-hoo back. He had his eyes closed and looked as green as an alien.

. . . **WHOOMPH!** They flew right out through the hole in the dome! The shock of the cold outdoor air stung Jake's eyes. He was still gaining speed. Eyes streaming, he gasped to see that he was rocketing straight towards a big wooden building . . . he could just make out the words **BUCKAROO BAR**—he was going to crash straight into it!

Jake screwed his eyes shut and waited for the bang—but then he felt his chair slowing down, slower . . . slower. . . and he came to a gentle stop.

A cowgirl was waiting to help them down.

'Howdy, folks!' she said, chirpily. 'Welcome to the Wild, Wild West Zone!'

Barnaby groaned. 'Fetch a bucket—I'm going to be sick!'

CHAPTER 8:

ROCKIN' ROGER'S RODEO BULL

'BLEEEEEEEEEEEEEUUUUURGH!'

Yuck. Barnaby's breakfast had come back up to say hello.

'Good thing I've got loads of buckets,' the cowgirl said to Jake as Barnaby groaned into his bucket. 'One of the kids who just came down tried to run off with three!'

'Which kid?' Jake asked, suddenly alert.

'Green furry costume, glasses. He's over there . . .'

She jerked her head towards the Buckaroo Bar. Sitting against the wall, with his head in a bucket, was Creature!

Every muscle in Jake's body tensed. He glanced at the cowgirl, but she had gone back to helping Barnaby. Looking up he saw Alexis and Karl whizzing down the zip wire, but he couldn't wait for them . . .

Jake took his coat off and tiptoed towards Creature.

Slowly, easy does it . . . Jake held his breath. *Closer . . . closer . . .*

'JAKE!'

A shout made him jump. *Alexis!* She and Karl were getting off the zip wire.

'Shhhh . . . ' Jake began, but it was too late.

Creature shot bolt upright, the bucket still on his head. With a tinny squeak, he bounded off . . .

CRASH!!

He bounced off the wall of the Buckaroo Bar, staggered to his feet and ran the other way.

DOOF!!!

Straight into Karl. Surprised, Karl tried to grab him, but Creature slipped through his fingers like a bar of slimy green soap.

'Surround him!' Jake shouted, just as Woodstock and Nora ran up.

Creature wrenched the bucket off his head and stood panting, his gloopy fur sticking out in all directions. Karl and Woodstock edged forward. Alexis and Nora edged forward. Jake edged forward . . .

'NOW!'

They pounced.

PAAAAAAAAAAAARP!

A cloud of lime green gas exploded from Creature's rear end, just as Jake hurled the coat over him. All five of them pinned the squawking Creature to the ground. After a minute, he stopped wriggling and started to make a rumbling noise.

Nora looked worried. 'Is he okay?'

'Maybe he's changing back!' Woodstock said, hopefully.

Jake peered under the coat. Creature was snoring.

'He's asleep,' Jake said, astonished.

'Ahhh—sweet!' Nora patted Jake's slimy, gloop-covered coat. Just then, Barnaby appeared.

'Where've you been?' Alexis asked, glaring at him. 'Running off again, I bet . . .'

Barnaby said nothing.

Jake saw that he still looked a bit green. 'He's here now, anyway,' he said quickly. 'More importantly, we have to think about how to get Creature to change back into Mr Hyde before one o'clock.'

'Sing to him? That worked before,' Karl suggested.

'Good idea. But we'll have to wake him up,' Jake said.

'Hey!' The cowgirl called over. 'There's a competition at Rockin' Roger's Rodeo to see who can stay on the bull the longest! It's behind the Buckaroo Bar . . .'

Alexis jumped up. 'I'll have a go!'

'How about Creature?!' Jake exclaimed.

'Well, we can't sing to him here,' Woodstock

said. 'People are staring . . . '

Jake looked round. Woodstock was right. He scooped Creature up.

'Okay—it might be quieter over there,' he said.

As they walked round the Buckaroo Bar, a cacophony of screaming hit Jake. In front of him was a circular arena with a life-size plastic bull in the middle. Around the edge were rows of shrieking kids. Jake stopped.

'This is a bad idea,' he said.

'Oh come on, Jake!' cried Alexis. 'Look— there are seats at the back . . . '

Before he could speak, Alexis ran down to the arena. Followed by the others, Jake reluctantly shuffled along the back row and sat down a couple of seats away from a scruffy-looking boy in a cowboy hat. The boy gave him a nod, then looked away.

Jake was about to put the coat-wrapped Creature on the seat next to him, but he paused. *Too risky—that boy might see him . . .* He tucked Creature carefully under his seat. As he sat back up, a loudspeaker crackled.

'Folks, our final contestant, with a time of fifty-nine seconds to beat . . . let's hear it for . . . Alexis 'Whipcrackin' Williams!'

There were cheers as Alexis ran into the arena. A cowboy handed her a cowboy hat as she climbed onto the bull. The bull started moving, slowly at first, but soon it was bucking madly. Jake held his breath, waiting for Alexis to be thrown off, but she stayed on, gripping the bull with one hand, waving her hat in the air with the other.

Ten seconds . . . twenty . . . thirty . . . Finally, Alexis was thrown off. There was a tense silence, as the cowboy studied his stopwatch.

'Sixty seconds preeeeeecisely! Ladies and Gentlemen, we have a winnerrrrrrrr!'

'GO ALEXIS!!' yelled Nora.

'Shhhh . . . you'll wake Creature!' Jake hissed. He put his hand under his seat and touched a Creature-shaped lump. *He's still asleep.*

The crowd cheered as the cowboy presented Alexis with a piece of paper. She bounded up the arena steps and, talking loudly at top speed, threw herself into the empty seat next to Jake.

'I WON! I WON! I won ice creams for us all!!!'

She high-fived Jake, then turned to the boy in the cowboy hat.

'I WON!' she exclaimed. 'Isn't that great?'

The boy shrugged.

Alexis looked at him, expectantly, hands on hips. She clearly felt this response was not good enough.

'Leave him alone, Alexis,' Jake whispered. The last thing they wanted was any more attention when they had Creature to deal with.

The boy looked up. 'Oh . . . look, I'm sorry. It *is* great. I'm just not having a good day . . . '

Alexis jumped up, still dizzy from her victory.

'What you need is ice cream! And I won free ones! Just wait here . . . ' She raced off.

Nora had been listening. She leaned over Jake and spoke to the boy.

'Why aren't you having a good day?' she asked.

'It doesn't matter,' he said. 'Anyway, I'm glad you guys seem to be enjoying yourselves.'

Nora was about to speak again, but then her eyes widened and she put her hand over her mouth.

'Oh . . . ' she whispered.

Jake slowly looked round.

Hovering vulture-like behind them was Mrs Blunt.

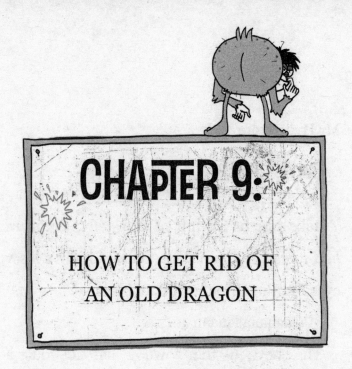

CHAPTER 9:

HOW TO GET RID OF AN OLD DRAGON

'I spy with my little eye,' Mrs Blunt said in a voice that sent a shiver up Jake's spine, 'Six pupils. But no Responsible Adult. Where, may I ask, is Mr Hyde?'

'In . . . the t-toilet, miss.' Nora's voice shook.

'Don't lie,' Mrs Blunt snapped. 'I have been informed that this group is wandering around without a teacher. Why would

Mr Hyde ignore my—'

PAAAAAAAAAAAAARP!

Jake caught a whiff of lime jelly. *Creature had farted . . . again!* He felt Mrs Blunt's laser eyes burning into the back of his head.

'Aaaaaaaaaaaaaah . . .'

The boy in the cowboy hat let out a long sigh.

Mrs Blunt's eyes swivelled round instantly. She marched along and rapped on the boy's hat.

'Did you just break wind?' Mrs Blunt screeched.

The boy stared. 'Break what?'

'QUIET! No one breaks wind in front of the Headteacher! It's Rule Number . . . Number . . . whatever number it is, you've earned a Sad

Face, young man.'

The boy looked confused. 'Sad Face?'

Mrs Blunt pulled a sheet of Sad Face stickers from her bag and slapped one on the boy's cowboy hat. She glared at the hat.

'And *what* is this monstrosity? That's not school dress code.'

SLAP. The hat got another sticker.

Jake tried to protest. 'Miss, he's not . . .'

'Silence, Jake Jones . . .'

Out of the corner of his eye, Jake spotted Alexis coming back with the ice creams. She stopped abruptly when she saw Mrs Blunt, who was still ranting.

' . . . and Barnaby McCrumb—you've earned yourself a day on the Rockery!'

Barnaby's head shot up. 'What've I done?!'

'You stole a pair of sunglasses from Amelia Trotter-Hogg.'

Barnaby's mouth dropped open. 'I found them!'

'He did, Miss,' Karl said.

'Amelia says he stole them,' Mrs Blunt snapped. 'And I trust her word.'

Jake stood up. Whatever Barnaby had done, he had NOT stolen the sunglasses. And Amelia had clearly forgotten to tell Mrs Blunt one thing . . .

'Miss,' Jake said. 'Did Amelia tell you that *she* was wandering about alone, without her group, when she lost her sunglasses?'

'Rubbish,' Mrs Blunt said, flustered. 'Amelia always sets a good example!'

'Loads of people saw her,' Nora added.

A thundercloud was forming just over Mrs Blunt's head.

'Nonsense. Well, Miss Trimble will be able to settle this, won't she! All of you, come with me—'

At that moment, Alexis ran forward.

'Guess what! I just saw that billionaire bloke, Wilfred Wibbly Whatzizname!!'

Mrs Blunt whirled round. The boy in the cowboy hat made an odd snorting noise.

'WHAT?! Wilfred Waldo Wellington? Where?!' Mrs Blunt exclaimed.

'In the Buckaroo Bar . . . he said he was going to the Flower Power Fairy Zone.'

'Flower Power . . . are you *sure?*' Mrs Blunt fluffed up her hair.

'Yes, Miss. He's giving out free ice creams! Would you like one?' Alexis asked.

'I've got more important things to think about,' snapped Mrs Blunt. 'Right—I have to get off . . . things to do, billionaires to see . . .'

Mrs Blunt stalked away.

'That got rid of the old dragon!' Alexis grinned. As she started handing out ice creams, the boy in the cowboy hat spoke.

'Can I—' he began.

'Of course!' Alexis held out an ice cream.

He shook his head, distracted. 'Oh, no thanks, I didn't mean—'

'More for me, then!' Barnaby tried to grab the ice cream. Alexis pushed his hand away.

'Get lost, Barnaby—'

'—Get lost!' The boy in the cowboy hat repeated. Who *isn't* lost?' he exclaimed. 'The maps are so bad, everywhere I go people are lost, lost, LOST! It's a disaster! No one will . . . wait . . . WHAT IS THAT?!'

He pointed to the arena. Jake looked, and his mouth dropped open.

The rodeo bull was starting to move. Perched on its back was Creature!

Everyone gasped. Jake leapt to his feet.

I should never have taken my eyes off him?!

The bull tipped forward.

'KIPPPERRRRRRRRRRR!'

With a Creaturish battle cry, Creature surfed along the bull's back and swung himself, by its horns, onto the head. The bull flung itself backwards.

Creature shot into the air, did three somersaults and landed on the bull's bottom.

'Ride 'em cowboy!' Barnaby whooped. Jake glared at him.

'Ta-dah,' Creature squawked smugly, and bowed. As he did so, the bull lurched again and Creature did three super-fast forward rolls along its back, landing back on the head. A look of enormous surprise crossed his face.

The boy in the cowboy hat roared with laughter.

The bull flung itself from side to side. Creature, clinging to one of the horns, whizzed round and round, faster and faster, till he was a furry blur.

'AH - AH - AH - AH - AAAAAAAARGH!' the furry blur gibbered.

The bull lurched forwards. With a shriek, Creature was flung high in the air . . .

'YEEEEEEEEEE-HA-A-A-A-AAA...OOMPH!'

He crash-landed in a cloud of dust, tried to stand up and fell over again, his eyes crossed.

'Now's our chance to grab him,' Jake murmured to Nora—but too late—Creature scrambled back on the bull.

'No kipper!' he said firmly. 'No kip . . . PER-R-R-RRRRRRRRRR!!!!'

The bull bucked violently, throwing Creature even higher. He landed with a clang on the roof of the bull-operating kiosk. This time he didn't try and get back on the bull, just crossed his arms and stared grumpily at it as it slowly ground to a halt.

The boy next to Jake wiped his eyes, shaking with laughter.

'That thing should be on TV!' he gasped. 'What *is* it?'

Jake thought quickly. 'He's—um—just one of the Alien Zone workers . . . '

The boy stopped laughing. His eyes narrowed.

'You're not telling me the truth. What's your name?' he demanded.

'Jake,' Jake said, uneasily.

The boy turned to Nora. 'And you?'

'I'm Nora,' she said. 'This is Alexis, Karl and Barnaby.'

The boy nodded. His face very thoughtful. *Why has he gone all grown up and formal?* Jake wondered. *Who is this kid?*

'And you are . . . ?' Jake asked.

The boy smiled.

'My name is Wilf.'

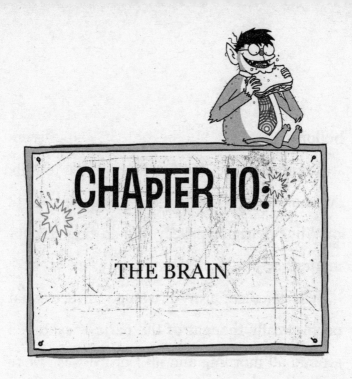

CHAPTER 10:

THE BRAIN

Nora, Karl, Alexis and Woodstock gasped. Jake's jaw dropped.

'*The* Wilf?' he stammered.

'Just "Wilf" is fine,' Wilf said, grinning.

The scruffy boy was none other than Wilfred Waldo Wellington Jnr., eccentric billionaire and owner of the adventure park!

Alexis looked doubtful. 'You don't *look* like a

billionaire!'

'I'm in disguise,' Wilf said. 'I wanted to walk around without anyone recognizing me.'

'Why?' Barnaby asked. 'Would they ask for money?'

Wilf laughed. 'No—I wanted to see what people really thought of the park. I wandered around all morning and all I heard was "we're lost . . . these maps are useless . . . !" So I came here to think what to do—but then you lot turned up, and your loopy Headteacher arrived, and that crazy creature appeared . . . speaking of which . . . '

Creature! Jake had almost forgotten about him! His eyes darted to the kiosk. Creature was still on the kiosk roof, sulking.

We have to catch him, he thought. *But that*

would mean telling Wilf...

'It is yours, isn't it?' Wilf said, watching Jake closely. 'I know it's not from the Alien Zone!'

There was a sudden wild cackle.

'Creature!' cried Nora. Jake turned to see Creature bounding out of the arena!

He jumped up. The others jumped up too.

'Sorry, Wilf—no time to explain . . .'

They raced back to the entrance of the arena, but Creature was already bouncing off into the distance. Jake started after him, but Wilf grabbed his arm.

'You'll never catch up,' Wilf said. 'Look—I can help you, but you have to tell me everything.'

Jake gulped. 'Okay . . .'

'You must swear not to tell anyone, though,' Nora said.

'I swear,' Wilf said.

'Well,' Jake said, slowly, 'Mr Hyde—our teacher—he sort of, well . . . he turns . . . '

Jake paused. 'Into a . . .'

'Creature!' finished Barnaby.

Wilf stared. 'That creature—is your teacher?!'

They all nodded. Jake looked at Wilf. *Will he be angry? Disbelieving? Laugh and think it a joke?*

But Wilf grabbed Jake's arm, an excited gleam in his eye.

'Really?!' he asked, breathlessly. 'How? Can anyone do it? Could *I* do it?!'

Jake was taken aback. 'Err . . . I don't think so.'

Wilf looked disappointed. 'Oh well. I'd like to have been able to change into a creature! So will he change back into a teacher?'

'Yes,' said Jake. 'But we've got to help him to do it before the Opening Ceremony at one o'clock! That's when the Head will see he's not there and we won't be able to cover that up . . . he'll lose his job.'

Wilf looked at his watch. 'It's half past eleven now. Okay, I've got an idea. Follow me.'

He ran to an electric golf cart that was parked at the back of the Buckaroo Bar.

'Jump in!' he called.

They all squished in. Wilf stepped on a pedal and the cart hummed smoothly off. Groups of people stepped out of their way and stared curiously at them as they went past.

'Creature went the other way!' Woodstock said.

'Trust me!' said Wilf, scooting round a corner. The cart came to a stop. 'Here we are.'

Jake looked up. A huge pink thing loomed before them. It looked like . . .

'A BRAIN!' exclaimed Nora. 'That's what that

pink blob on the map was!'

Wilf flushed. 'I know—I'm hopeless at drawing.'

'How did you design the park, then?' asked Woodstock.

'You'll see in a minute,' said Wilf, jumping down from the cart. 'This is the Brain—my control centre. Come on . . . '

Following Wilf into the Brain, they found themselves in a huge, brightly lit room. One wall was a bank of screens. In the middle of the room was a round pit filled with LEGO bricks, and to one side of this stood a complicated LEGO structure. Jake walked over and saw it was a perfect model of the whole park.

'Awesome!' said Woodstock. He got out his sketchbook and started doodling.

'That's how I designed the park,' said Wilf. 'But there's no time . . . GENIE!'

A silver robot came gliding towards them.

'Hi Wilf,' said the robot. 'What is your wish?'

'Cameras please,' said Wilf. Immediately, the wall of screens flickered into life.

'There are cameras all over the park,' explained Wilf. 'If we look for long enough, we should be able to find your creature . . . teacher.'

They spread out along the wall and stared at the screens. On one screen, Jake spotted Mrs Blunt chasing a smartly dressed man carrying ice creams. But no Creature—

'Here!' yelled Karl.

Everyone rushed over.

All Jake could see on the screen was a wailing

child holding an empty hotdog bun.

'Where?'

Creature's face suddenly appeared on the next screen. He was covered in ketchup and a hotdog was hanging out of his mouth. He slurped it in, burped at the camera and disappeared again.

Jake shook his head. 'We've lost him.'

'No we haven't!' cried Alexis, pointing at another screen.

A bald man was clutching his head and waving his fist. Two seconds later, on the next screen, Creature appeared—now wearing a wig.

Barnaby fell about laughing. Nora groaned. 'He's being naughtier than ever!'

Wilf spoke to the robot.

'Two walkie-talkies, please, Genie!'

'Your wish is my command,' said the robot, gliding off.

Wilf turned to Jake.

'You take a walkie-talkie and go after Creature. I'll take one and watch the screens. Then I can tell you right where he's got to.'

'Great idea!' said Alexis.

'We'll need maps, though,' said Jake.

Wilf hit himself on the head. 'But you can't use the maps! You'll get lost . . .'

'No we won't!'

Everyone looked round. Woodstock was holding up his sketchbook.

Wilf blinked. 'What's that?'

'A map of the park,' said Woodstock, handing it to Wilf. 'Only with everything in the right place.'

'But how . . . ' Wilf looked flabbergasted.

'Easy—I just copied the LEGO model,' said Woodstock.

'Easy?! I wouldn't be able to . . . anyway, it's brilliant!'

Woodstock flushed with pride.

Wilf handed Woodstock's map to the robot, who had just returned with the walkie-talkies.

'Quick Genie—six copies of this please. We've got a Creature to catch!!'

CHAPTER 11:

MONKEY MAYHEM

Jake and his friends sprinted out of the Brain.

'It's 12.30 now,' said Nora. 'We've got half an hour.'

Wilf's voice crackled over Jake's walkie-talkie.

'Jake—can you hear me?'

Jake pushed the 'Talk' button. 'Yes . . .'

'Creature's in the Wildlife Zone, heading for Monkey Mayhem. Can you see it on the map?'

Nora peered at her map. 'Got it!'

Following the map, they soon came to a building with a roof shaped like a banana. A sign read:

MONKEYMAYHEM

'There's another entrance at the back,' Woodstock said, pointing at the map.

'We'll have more chance of catching him if we split up,' Alexis said.

'Okay,' Jake said. 'Three of us will go in this way . . . '

'I'll come with you,' Nora said.

Woodstock stepped forward. 'Me too.'

Karl looked at Alexis and Barnaby. 'We'll go round the back, then.'

As Karl, Alexis and Barnaby disappeared, Nora pushed the door open. Jake groaned.

'It's just like a jungle!'

It was as if they had walked into a tropical rainforest. Huge trees towered on every side, and from their branches swung a chattering rabble of monkeys.

'He could be anywhere!' said Nora. 'This is not good.'

'Worse—look who's turned up,' said Woodstock.

Heading towards them from the other end of the monkey house was Amelia's group. It was too late to run or hide. Amelia had spotted them.

'OY! Jake Jones!'

Amelia charged towards Jake like a rampaging rhino.

'WHY DID YOU TELL ON ME TO MRS BLUNT?' she shrieked.

Several monkeys fell out of their trees in fright. Jake opened his mouth to speak, but at that moment Miss Trimble hurried up with the rest of the group.

'Now, children, I'm sure this can be resolved

by non-violent means . . . '

SPLAT!!!

A large rotten mango fell out of a tree and exploded on Amelia's head.

'Aaaaaargh!' she screamed.

SQUELCH! SQUISH! SPLAT!

Jake jumped back as several more mangoes splatted down on Amelia's group. One landed on the unfortunate Miss Trimble's head and was

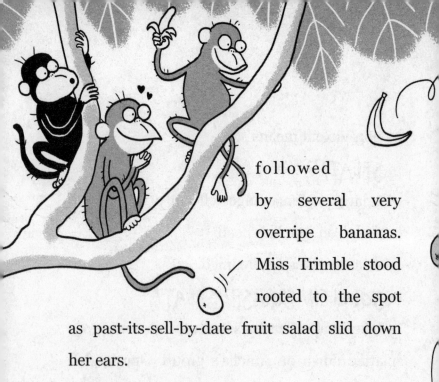

followed by several very overripe bananas. Miss Trimble stood rooted to the spot as past-its-sell-by-date fruit salad slid down her ears.

She sank to the floor.

'Ohhhhhh . . . ' she moaned. 'I think I'm having one of my funny turns . . . '

Amelia stood quivering with fury, mango juice dribbling down her face. Jake, Nora and Woodstock dodged through the rain of fruit to help Miss Trimble.

'Is it the End of the World, children?' she asked in a quavering voice.

'No, Miss, it's a monkey throwing mangoes,' said Jake, hauling her to her feet. A few metres away, a huge palm leaf jutted out over the path.

'Under there!' he said.

They bundled Miss Trimble under the shelter of the palm leaf. Jake peered out. Through the leaves, he could just see the monkey who was throwing fruit.

It was a very large, greenish monkey, and it was wearing glasses and a wig. Thanks to the green gloop he was well camouflaged by the leaves.

'That's no monkey up there, that's Creature!'

Jake hissed to Woodstock and Nora.

Several real monkeys were perched a few branches away, gazing at Creature in stupefied awe.

Amelia gave a yelp and ducked as another banana whizzed past her ear.

She picked up the banana and threw it back to where Creature and the monkeys were sitting. Immediately, Creature's fan club of monkeys launched a barrage of bananas in her direction.

'HELP!!!!' she screamed, fending off the hail of fruit.

Jake grabbed her too and pulled her under the leaf. Then he spotted Karl and Alexis coming through the back door and running towards them.

'What's going on?!' exclaimed Alexis, looking round in astonishment.

'Monkeys throwing fruit. Where's Barnaby?' said Jake.

Karl looked around. 'He came in through a side door. He should be here . . . '

Amelia crossed her arms. 'So now there's no Barnaby and there's no Mr Hyde? Just wait till I tell Mrs Blunt!'

She barged out from under the leaf. 'Come on, my group . . . '

Amelia's group filed after her. But Miss Trimble didn't move. She was still sitting under the palm leaf, talking to a banana. Amelia came marching back.

'Come on, Miss!' she snapped. 'We've got to find Mrs Blunt!'

Miss Trimble peered up at her. 'Blunt? Well sharpen it, dear!'

Amelia stared. 'I said "Mrs Blunt!" Have you got mango in your ear?'

Miss Trimble spluttered. 'What?! My rear is just fine, thank you.'

'YOUR EAR!!' shouted Amelia. 'Oh, let's just go . . .'

She marched back towards the door.

Woodstock and Nora helped Miss Trimble up. She smiled vaguely at them, and held up her banana.

'This is Boris,' she said. 'He's going to help me make banana custard!'

Jake and the others watched, as she tottered off after Amelia, leaving a trail of mango juice behind her.

'She's gone a bit loopy—fruit loopy!' said Karl.

Alexis giggled.

'Don't be mean. Should we go with her?' asked Nora. Two Class 5a pupils were helping Miss Trimble out of the door.

'Her group will look after her,' said Jake. 'We've got to catch Creature—'

Karl looked at his watch. 'And we've only fifteen minutes to do it!'

'Come on, then!' Jake turned towards the tree where Creature had been.

Creature and his fan club had vanished. But Barnaby was leaning against the trunk, a mischievous grin on his face.

'Barnaby!' exclaimed Nora. 'Where *were* you?!'

Barnaby shrugged. 'I didn't want to get mangoed, so I hid behind a tree.'

Jake was furious. 'You could have helped us out!'

'Jake stood up for you to Mrs Blunt earlier,' Woodstock said.

Barnaby's grin faded. Jake thought he looked a bit guilty.

'Oh—yeah. Sorry . . . '

Alexis glared at him. 'We have to work together, Barnaby, or we'll never catch Creature.'

Just then, Wilf's voice crackled over Jake's walkie-talkie.

'Jake! You've got to get to the Crocodile Pool! Creature's trying to feed bananas to the crocodile!'

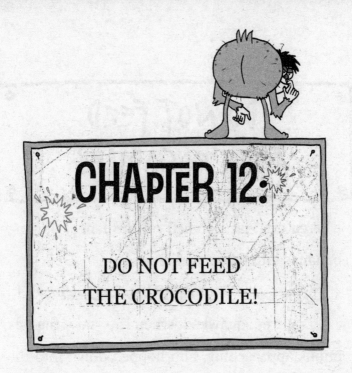

CHAPTER 12:

DO NOT FEED
THE CROCODILE!

'Come on!' Alexis sped off, Jake and the others hot on her heels. They burst out of the monkey house.

'Which way, Nora?' Woodstock shouted.

She scanned the map. 'Straight on!'

In a couple of minutes they reached a high wire fence with a large sign on it.

DO NOT FEED THE CROCODILE!

Creature was perched on the fence, flinging bananas into the crocodile pool.

'Wheeeeee . . . ' PLOP! 'Wheeeeee . . . '

Creature squawked when he saw the six pupils approaching, and hopped down into the enclosure.

'GET OUT, CREATURE!' yelled Jake, slamming against the fence.

'Do you want to be lunch?!' shouted Alexis. 'There's a crocodile in there!'

Creature cackled, stuck two bananas in his ears and bounded to the pool. A huge gnarled log was floating in it. Creature hurled himself onto one end of the log, causing it to rock dangerously.

Creature laughed, and bounced up and down.

'BOING! BOING! BOING!'

Then he stood on one leg and pretended to be a ballet dancer.

'Tra-la-laaaa ... ahhhhhh ...' Creature's eyes widened. He looked down.

'... aaaaaaaaaaaaaHHHHH!!!!'

The end of the log where Creature was pirouetting was rising into the air!

'ARR-AAAAR-R-R-R?!?' croaked the log.

'THE LOG!' shouted Karl. 'IT'S A CROCODILE!!!!'

Everyone screamed. Jake's legs turned to jelly.
Creature was pirouetting on the huge scaly nose
of the biggest crocodile Jake had ever seen!

The crocodile's yellow eyes fixed on Creature.

Creature chattered noisily. He pulled the
bananas out of his ears . . .

Nora shouted. 'Whatever you do . . . '

. . . and stuck them in the crocodile's cave-
like nostrils.

'Don't make it angry!'

**'AR-AR-AR-ARRAAAARRRR-R-
R-R-R-R-R!!!'**

The crocodile made a noise like a T. Rex
that had swallowed a power drill. It jerked its
head back, tossing Creature and the bananas
into the air. Then, with a powerful flick of
its tail, it whacked Creature right across the

enclosure. The six friends watched, horrified, as he slammed against the fence on the other side and slid to the ground in a daze.

The crocodile glided through the water towards Creature.

He'll be eaten alive! There was only one thing for it.

Jake scrambled up the fence.

'What are you doing?' shouted Karl.

'I'm going in,' Jake shouted, jumping over. 'I'll distract it, get it to come this way . . .'

Nora scrambled over too.

'I'm coming,' she said. 'I'll try to talk to it . . .'

'Nora—you can't *talk* to a croc!'

'*I* can. Come on . . .'

They ran to the pool. The crocodile was crawling up the bank towards Creature.

'OVER HERE!' shouted Jake.

The crocodile kept crawling.

Jake swallowed. *I'll have to get closer.* The pool looked shallow enough. He stepped in, and sank up to his waist in cold, muddy water.

'Aaarrrrahhhh-ah-ah-ahhhh!' croaked Nora.

The crocodile looked round.

'What did you say?' hissed Jake.

'"We are your friends," I think . . . I've only ever tested it on frogs though . . .'

With a sharp turn, the crocodile slid back into the water and began to glide straight towards Jake!

'I don't *want* to be its friend!' panted Jake, trying to clamber out. But his foot had got tangled up in pondweed! Blood started to pound painfully in his ears.

'I'm stuck!'

'Grab my hand!' Nora cried. Jake grabbed it. Nora pulled . . . Jake felt his foot break free . . .

'Aaaaaaaaaaaaaaargh!!'

Nora's feet shot out from under her! With a scream, she plunged into the pool and disappeared under the water. Jake heaved her up, floundering and gasping. A few metres away, he could see the crocodile getting closer . . . and closer . . .

'KIPPPPPPPPPPPPERRRRRRRRR!!!'

A brown furball landed—WHUMP!—on the tip of the crocodile's nose. Nora gasped.

'Creature!'

'AAARRRRR?!' The crocodile grunted in shock. He swung his head from side to side in a frenzy, trying to shake Creature off. But Creature

had learned a few tricks from the rodeo bull! He hung on, hollering like a cowboy.

'Yeeee-hawwwwwww!'

The crocodile got angrier and angrier, lashing the water up into a muddy froth.

We have to get out! With a massive effort, Jake tried to heave Nora up the bank, but she kept on slipping back down . . .

SNAP!

The crocodile's mouth snapped shut. Jake and Nora whirled round.

Creature was nowhere to be seen.

'You bully! You ate him!' screamed Nora.

The crocodile began to open its mouth again. But at that moment a small, bedraggled, bespectacled cannonball burst out of the water and threw itself towards Jake and Nora.

'Kipppppeerrrrrrrrrrrrr!!' Creature growled at the crocodile.

Jake gaped. *He's protecting us!* This scraggy little bundle of mischief was standing up to a monster crocodile—for him and Nora! *What was it that Mr Hyde had said about friends . . . ?*

The crocodile's eyes gleamed. Then it surged towards Creature.

'FRIENDS STICK TOGETHER!' Jake shouted. He and Nora charged at the crocodile and grabbed Creature. Jake raised a fist. 'Get out of here, you overgrown lizard!' he cried.

The crocodile didn't seem to like being called an overgrown lizard. It started to open its mouth and lunged forwards . . . Jake closed his eyes . . .

'CROCCY! BICCIES!'

Jake's eyes snapped open. He saw Barnaby and Karl on one side of the pool, hurling biscuits at the crocodile.

The crocodile stopped moving, confused.

Then there was a shout. 'HEY!!'

Jake whirled round—Alexis and Woodstock were on the other side of the pool, beating sticks together and yelling at the top of their lungs.

The crocodile swung its head from side to side—not sure where to look. It gave a low groan.

'Keep going, everyone!' shouted Jake. 'I think it's working! We're really confusing him.'

They carried on. As the crocodile became more and more disorientated, Jake felt warmth coming off the soggy Creature.

Nora gasped. 'He's glowing!'

It was true. Creature was bathed in orange

light. Soon, every hair on his body was glowing. Sparks flew off him.

'OW!' Jake and Nora let go of the now red-hot Creature, who rolled back into the water.

CRACK!!

A bolt of lightning shot out from his tail and struck the crocodile on the nose.

'AAA-AAAA-AAAARGGGH!!' roared the crocodile. Its nose smoking, the huge reptile turned and slipped under the surface of the pool.

The water frothed and churned . . . the smell of burning rubber filled the air . . .

FAAAAAAAAAAAAAARRRRRRT!

Wheeeeeeee . . . .

POP! POP! POP!

BANG!

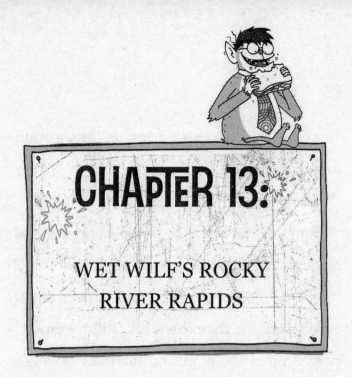

CHAPTER 13:

WET WILF'S ROCKY RIVER RAPIDS

'Jake, Nora! Grab these!'

Karl, Barnaby, Woodstock and Alexis were at the top of the bank, pushing branches down to the water. Jake and Nora grabbed them and were dragged, shaken and dripping, up the slope.

'Creature's changed!' Jake managed to gasp as he collapsed onto the bank.

'Yeah,' said Barnaby, grinning. 'It was quite a show!'

Karl pointed. Jake turned.

Standing knee deep in steaming mud was Mr Hyde, muddy but back to normal. He took off his muddy glasses, wiped them on his muddy jacket and put them back on, still muddy. He peered up at the pupils on the bank staring at him. Then he looked down at himself.

'Oh no,' he groaned. 'I didn't do anything too . . . silly—did I?'

Jake paused. 'Well . . . '

He was saved from answering by a shout.

'CONAN! Where's Conan?!'

Jake turned, to see Wilf running towards them.

'Who's Conan?!' asked Woodstock, puzzled.

Wilf screeched to a halt beside them.

'The crocodile,' he panted. 'Conan is completely harmless—he's got no teeth!'

Everyone stared.

'No teeth?' spluttered Nora. 'How did we not notice that?!'

Jake laughed. 'You normally notice everything!'

Nora looked miffed. 'I was a teensy bit terrified, remember?'

Wilf looked mortified. 'I tried to tell you over the walkie-talkie but it went dead! It must have got water in it!' He looked round. 'Where is he?'

Alexis pointed. 'Over there.'

The terrified, toothless crocodile had left the water and was hiding behind a tree on the far bank.

Wilf turned to Jake. 'Sorry—I should have told you earlier. We're having a set of false teeth made for him, but at the moment all he can eat is soup!'

'Ahem . . . could someone give me a hand, please?'

A soggy Mr Hyde was trying to climb out of the pool. Together, they pulled him up the bank.

'So you're the one who can turn into a creature!' said Wilf, gazing wonderingly at the teacher. Mr Hyde gave Jake a worried look.

'Sir, this is Wilf, the park owner,' said Jake.

'He swore not to tell on you,' said Nora, giving Wilf a stern look.

'I won't,' said Wilf. His walkie-talkie suddenly crackled. He picked it up. 'Genie?'

A robotic voice spoke:

'Opening ceremony in five minutes.'

Jake slapped his head. *The Opening Ceremony!* He'd almost forgotten it, in all the chaos.

'We've got to go!' he cried. 'I'd rather face a croc than Mrs Blunt if we're not there at one o'clock!'

'We won't make it,' groaned Karl. 'We're

miles from the entrance!'

Wilf looked thoughtful. 'There might be a way . . .'

He ran to the fence and climbed over. Mystified, Jake and his friends followed. Wilf pointed to a gate just across from the crocodile enclosure.

A sign over the gate read:

WET WILF'S
ROCKY RIVER RAPIDS

'The fastest ride in the park,' said Wilf, proudly. 'It goes round the edge of the Wildlife Zone—and finishes at the entrance!'

'Genius!' exclaimed Woodstock.

They ran through the gate and up a flight of steps, emerging next to a narrow channel of water, with canoes bobbing in a line. At the end was a sudden drop, from which came the sound of rushing water.

Wilf began unhooking canoes.

'Nora, Alexis—you first,' he said. They jumped in the first canoe and Wilf gave it a mighty shove. Jake heard screams as they disappeared.

Barnaby and Karl got in the next one. Jake helped push them, whooping, over the edge.

'Jake and Mr Hyde, you next!'

Jake helped his teacher into the canoe and jumped into the front seat. Wilf and Woodstock pushed the canoe out.

Even under his layer of mud, Mr Hyde looked pale.

'Hold tight, sir,' shouted Jake. 'WHOA . . . '

For one heart-stopping moment, the canoe teetered on the brink . . .

SPLOOSH!!

The canoe slammed into the water and plunged down what seemed like an almost vertical drop!

'OOOOOOOHHHHHHH!!' yelled Mr Hyde. The bottom was coming up towards them, fast—too fast! Jake crouched lower in his seat and covered his head, holding his breath . . .

WHUMP! A wall of water hit the canoe. Jake felt it wash over him.

'Gleuuuurgghhhh!' gurgled Mr Hyde, who hadn't ducked. The front of the canoe was underwater . . . *they were going to capsize!* But by some miracle, the canoe righted itself . . . Jake barely had time to take a breath when the canoe veered sharply to one side. *Ouch!* His neck twisted. The canoe swung back the other way. The banks were getting higher and higher. They were being sucked into a dark, narrow gorge. Sharp rocks reared up out of the water ahead.

'Are we nearly there yet?' he heard Mr Hyde yell, his voice echoing off the steep walls.

'I don't know!' Jake yelled back.

The canoe rocketed along, faster and faster, dodging the rocks with millimetres to spare. The gorge got narrower and narrower. Then Jake gasped—straight ahead was a huge rock!

They were going to crash right into it!

Jake closed his eyes. Five . . . four . . . three . . . two . . . one . . .

But the crash never came. Jake opened his eyes just in time to see the rock split open, straight down the middle! The canoe shot through and Jake found they were floating gently along a calm, narrow channel. The canoe slowly came to rest beside a wooden platform.

Nora, Alexis, Karl and Barnaby ran to help him and Mr Hyde out.

'Mr Hyde, you're clean again!' exclaimed Nora.

It was true. Mr Hyde was dripping wet like the rest of them, but there was no longer a trace of mud or green gloop on him.

'Come on,' called Alexis. 'It's two minutes to one!'

'Hang on, here come Wilf and Woodstock,' said Jake. The rock opened again, and the last canoe shot through and floated up to the platform.

There was no one in it!

CHAPTER 14:

THE GRAND
OPENING CEREMONY

They stared at the empty canoe.

'They must have fallen out!' gasped Nora.

Jake peered upriver, but the rock had closed, blocking his view.

Mr Hyde clutched his head and groaned. 'This is a disaster! We'll have to go back—'

'Wait—what's this?' Jake fished a piece of paper from the bottom of the empty canoe. It looked like a page from Woodstock's sketchbook.

Everyone crowded round as he unfolded it.

'It just says "Go!"' said Jake.

'So let's go, then!' said Barnaby.

Jake tugged a reluctant Mr Hyde through the gate. Ahead, he saw the Space Port building where they had first come in. A crowd of excited people swarmed around a podium which had been placed to one side of it. At the front, Jake spotted Mrs Blunt, glaring as she scanned the area.

Looking for Mr Hyde, Jake thought. He grabbed his teacher's arm, and they pushed through the crowd. As they neared Mrs Blunt, Jake heard a shrill voice.

'THERE THEY ARE MISS! I bet Mr Hyde's not . . .'

Amelia's voice faltered.

'Hello, Amelia,' said Mr Hyde, cheerily.

'MR HYDE!' exploded Mrs Blunt. 'Why haven't you been with your group all day?!'

'He has, Miss,' said Jake. 'He just had to, um—go to the loo . . . '

' . . . a lot,' finished Barnaby.

Mr Hyde cottoned on. 'Yes—must have been something I ate.' There was a loud rumble. He looked pained. 'Oh dear! That only happens when I have awful wind . . . '

Mrs Blunt turned pale and backed away. 'Please! I've heard enough.'

'Miss, Miss . . . ' Amelia was jumping up and down, trying to get Mrs Blunt's attention. 'There's a pupil missing . . . '

At that moment, the crowd gave an excited gasp. 'Ooooooooooh . . . '

Everyone was pointing at the sky. Jake looked up and saw a huge W-shaped hang-glider floating towards them. Suspended beneath it were two figures in helmets and goggles.

As it came closer, Jake gasped. *Was it . . .?*

'W for Wilf!' shouted Barnaby.

'And W for Woodstock!' laughed Nora.

The W swooped lower. Even though the two figures were helmeted, Jake could see that they were, indeed, Wilf and Woodstock! Wilf called through a megaphone.

'GREETINGS, EVERYONE! WELCOME TO MY ADVENTURE PARK!'

The hang-glider circled lower and lower till it landed with a gentle bump in front of the podium. There was a ripple of applause.

Wilf and Woodstock started to unstrap themselves.

'MISTER WELLINGTON!!'

Mrs Blunt was barging her way through the crowd.

'It *is* Mr Wellington, isn't it?' she said, stopping in front of Wilf and looking him up and down.

He nodded, slightly reluctantly Jake thought. 'Yes . . . that's me.'

'I thought you'd be taller . . . anyway, I *do* hope you remember me,' she went on. 'My name is Mrs Blunt. I wrote asking if you could donate some money towards an exciting project for my humble little school? Some of the pupils have already raised quite a lot, young Woodstock, for example . . . where is he . . .?'

Woodstock took off his helmet and goggles. Mrs Blunt looked surprised.

'Well, I see you two have met! Woodstock, tell Mr Wellington about our worthy cause . . . '

Woodstock looked Mrs Blunt straight in the eye.

'Mrs Blunt, I've explained to Wilf. *I* collected money for a new art studio. But *you* want to put it towards a load of boring statues of headteachers!'

'Oh dear . . . ' murmured the crowd.

Mrs Blunt began to flush red.

Wilf pulled his goggles up, and looked at Mrs Blunt.

'I *do* remember you,' he said. 'You're the lady who accused me of farting.'

'Oh dear . . . ' gasped the crowd, louder.

Mrs Blunt's eyes bulged.

'YOU?!' she spluttered. 'That—that scruffy boy at Rockin' Roger's Rodeo? *You* are Wilfred Waldo Wellington Jnr.?'

'Just "Wilf" is fine,' said Wilf. 'Now, if you'll excuse me . . .'

He climbed onto the podium and spoke into a microphone.

'Welcome to the Grand Opening of Wacky Wilf's Wild Adventure Park! I know there have been problems with the maps today and I want to put that right. May I introduce my new map-making assistant—WOODSTOCK STONE!'

'HURRAY!' yelled the crowd.

Woodstock looked almost as shocked as Mrs Blunt.

'M-me?' he gasped.

Wilf hadn't finished. 'It's a paid job. I'll triple the money you've raised for the art studio . . . '

Woodstock's eyes nearly popped out.

' . . . but the money has to go towards an art studio, not statues.'

'HURRAY AGAIN!' The crowd went wild.

Mrs Blunt didn't go wild. She went a ghastly shade of white.

'And if it's okay with you, I'd love to design the art studio myself—with some help from my friends,' said Wilf, grinning cheekily at Jake and the others.

He turned, then turned back. 'Nearly forgot.

I declare this park to be . . . OPEN!'

Wilf ran to join Jake and the others. Mr Hyde clapped him on the back. 'Marvellous gesture, young Wilf.'

A band suddenly started playing loud, funky music. Mr Hyde's eyes lit up.

'Wonderful—I love a boogie!'

Wilf's eyes widened as Mr Hyde started twitching like a giraffe being attacked by killer bees.

'Who wants to dance?' cried Mr Hyde. He spotted Miss Trimble. She was wandering around in a daze, telling everyone her secret recipe for banana custard.

'Three eggs . . . '

'Miss Trimble! Care for a dance?'

She peered at him. 'A spoonful of sugar . . .'

Mr Hyde grabbed Miss Trimble.

'Helps the medicine go down!' sang Mr Hyde.
He whirled her round so her feet flew up in
the air.

'Then . . . add . . . bananas . . . ' gasped Miss Trimble, whizzing round faster and faster.

'Look!' Nora nudged Jake. He turned to see Mrs Blunt being helped to a bench by park staff. Amelia was running alongside her.

'MISS! You've got to do something, Miss! Why don't you . . .?'

Jake grinned at Nora. She was about to say something, when . . .

Fizzzzzzzzzzz . . . POP!!

The crowd ooohed. 'Fireworks!'

'Fireworks? In the daytime?' Nora said, puzzled.

POP! POP! POP!

Jake sniffed. *Those fireworks smell odd— kind of like . . . burning rubber?* He spun round.

'That's not fireworks! That's . . . '

'BANANA CUSTAAAAAAAAAAAAAAAARD!' shrieked Miss Trimble, flying through the air. Mr Hyde's coat lay in a steaming pile on the ground.

Jake and Nora looked at each other in horror.

'Oh no! Not again, Mr Hyde!'

SCHOOL REPORTS

JAKE JONES

JAKE JONES
REPORT SUMMARY

Jake is undoubtedly one of life's high fliers! On a recent school trip, his zest on a zip wire was matched only by his courage in fending off brain-munching zombies and killer crocodiles. Jake has a strong sense of right and wrong and will stand by his friends through thick and thin. He is a great person to have around in a crisis as he has the ability to keep his head, although in a recent situation I must admit he was in some danger of losing an arm or leg. But life probably won't throw Jake in too many croc pools—we hope!

SIGNED: Mr E. Hyde

BARNABY McCRUMB

BARNABY McCRUMB
REPORT SUMMARY

Barnaby has shown great acting potential—throwing himself into the role of 'Head Zombie' with relish. Specifically, tomato relish. I feel that Barnaby would do very well in a zombie apocalypse, since in the classroom it's often not clear if he's dead or alive. One of Barnaby's goals has been to try harder to focus on tasks. He has made progress here, but he now needs to apply this skill to something other than playing games on his phone.

SIGNED: Mr E. Hyde

NORA NEWTON
REPORT SUMMARY

Nora is making excellent progress in all subject areas, particularly science, which is her main passion. I was delighted when she told me recently that she was learning a language. I was slightly less delighted to discover that it was not French or Spanish, since these are the ones the government seems to want children to learn, but Crocodilian. I am not quite sure how I am supposed to test her progress, since I do not speak Crocodilian. However, I'm sure it will be extremely useful to her when she becomes David Attenborough, which is her stated chosen career path.

NORA NEWTON

SIGNED: Mr E. Hyde

WOODSTOCK STONE REPORT SUMMARY

Woodstock's artistic confidence has rocketed sky high after he redrew all the maps for a local adventure park. The classroom is now covered from floor to ceiling in maps. Whilst wishing to encourage his creativity, I have had to remind him several times that the other pupils do not need a map to get to the toilet. Woodstock recently asked if we can combine art lessons with hang-gliding, as he believes it will help him draw maps of the surrounding countryside. I'm afraid I said something like 'Not on your Nelly.'

SIGNED: Mr E. Hyde

KARL McQUEEN REPORT SUMMARY

Karl's passion for drama was rekindled by events on our recent school trip. He is now working on a new musical entitled 'How to Tame Your Crocodile'. It features music (written by Karl) including a number called 'Let Me Go', which he, worryingly, thinks will 'go viral'. His confidence is admirable, but I'm not sure we want to spread infectious diseases around. I have suggested that he involves at least one other pupil, since playing all the main parts seems a little over-optimistic, even for Karl.

SIGNED: Mr E. Hyde

ALEXIS WILLIAMS

ALEXIS WILLIAMS
REPORT SUMMARY

Alexis is a sports-mad pupil who likes to take the bull by the horns in any challenge—literally! This term she has won trophies for football, netball, basketball, table tennis, crazy golf and tiddlywinks. Her latest passion is for rodeo. She has bought a large Stetson hat, says 'howdy' a lot and sings country and western songs till the cows come home. I have tried to explain to Alexis the obvious health and safety problems to having a bull on the school premises, but she doesn't seem to understand the common English phrase: 'It's too dangerous'.

SIGNED: Mr E. Hyde

CREATURE

CREATURE
REPORT SUMMARY

Creature is coming along in leaps and bounds! Particularly with his Leaping and Bounding skills. Other areas he shows talent in are Causing Havoc, Wreaking Mayhem and Running Amok. He has also displayed an interest in Crocodile Rodeo, Chandelier Dismantling and Fruit Hurling. Yes, I know these are not actually curriculum subjects, but if they were, Creature would be Top of the Class. Areas in which Creature could improve include—well, most other areas, actually. However, he does seem to have the ability to inspire fanatical loyalty in both humans and monkeys—a rare gift and one to be worked on.

SIGNED: Mr E. Hyde

MR HYDE
REPORT SUMMARY

MR HYDE

Mr Hyde is the Best Teacher In The Universe! He's not like a normal teacher, he's more like a very tall kid with nose hair. He's really good at playing the ~~yucalally~~ ukulele. He knows all the words and actions to Agadoo although his singing is a bit iffy. He dances like an octopus with itchy tentacles (except octopuses have eight tentacles and Mr Hyde only has four). He is scared of zombies and gets stressed out sometimes and then he does this thing—oh yeah, we're not supposed to tell you that bit...

SIGNED: Nora Newton Jake Jones

AMELIA TROTTER-HOGG
REPORT SUMMARY

AMELIA TROTTER-HOGG

What can I say? Amelia is practically perfect at virtually everything. She reminds me of myself at that age. She reminds me of herself constantly, too—wherever I look, there she is, looking as pristine as ever, bearing a gift for me of some sort! Amelia is refreshingly aware of her own brilliance. She is also very keen to point out other pupils' faults and failings, and to help them put these right of course—such a kind, thoughtful child. Keep up the good work, Amelia!

SIGNED: Mrs Blunt

POP!

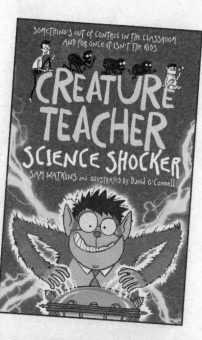

SOMETHING'S OUT OF CONTROL IN THE CLASSROOM...
AND FOR ONCE IT ISN'T THE KIDS

CREATURE TEACHER
SCIENCE SHOCKER

SAM WATKINS and ILLUSTRATED BY David O'Connell

Creature Teacher Science Shocker

One creature is hard to handle. But two? That's DOUBLE TROUBLE! Jake's class are competing in the Whizz-BANG Science Fair and surely nothing can stop them from winning at the final. Well, maybe one thing... ...their teacher, Mr Hyde, has turned into Creature, and is more interested in eating the exhibits than talking about them. And what's more, Creature's made a friend! With two mischievous monsters causing havoc, things are about to get EXPLOSIVE!

About the author

Sam Watkins voraciously consumed books from a young age, due to a food shortage in the village where she grew up. This diet, although not recommended by doctors, has given her a lifelong passion for books. She has been a bookseller, editor and publisher, and writes and illustrates her own children's books. At one point, things all got a bit too bookish so she decided to be an art teacher for a while, but books won the day in the end.

About the illustrator

David O'Connell is an illustrator who lives in London. His favourite things to draw are monsters, naughty children (another type of monster), batty old ladies, and evil cats . . . Oh, and teachers that transform into naughty little creatures!

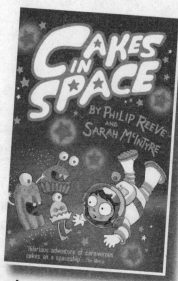

Here are some other stories
that we think you'll love.